Complimentary

Another Sommer-Time Story™

The UGLY Caterpillar

By Carl Sommer

Illustrated by Greg Budwine

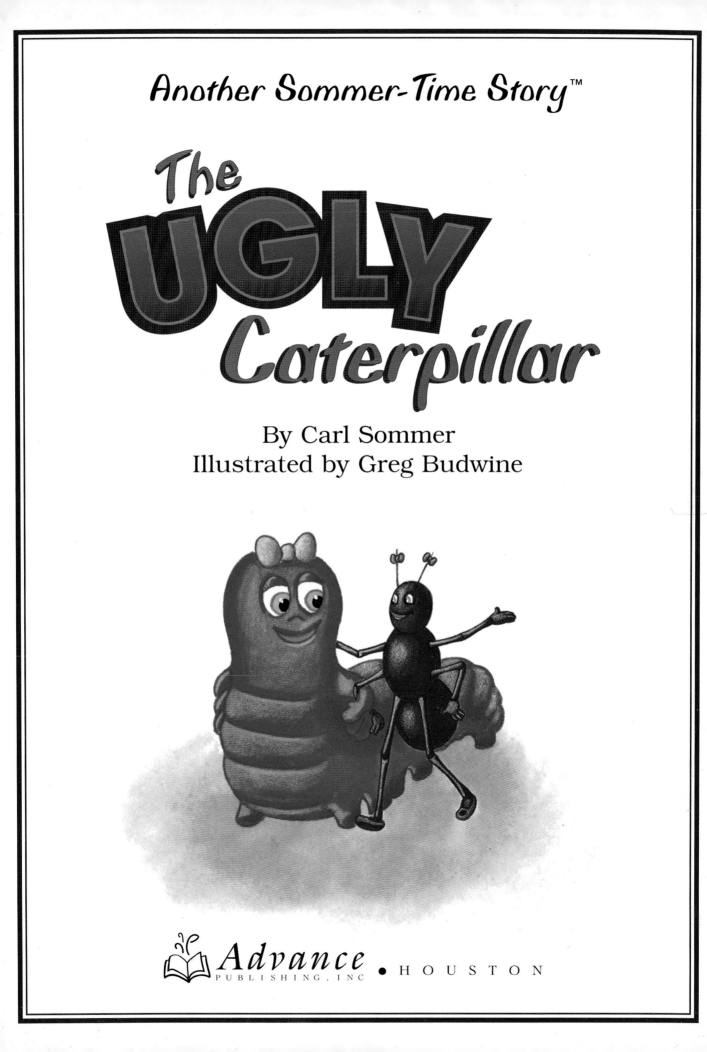

Advance PUBLISHING, INC • HOUSTON

Permissions
Advance Publishing, Inc.
6950 Fulton St.
Houston, TX 77022

www.advancepublishing.com

First Edition
Printed in Singapore

Library of Congress Cataloging-in-Publication Data

Sommer, Carl, 1930-
 The Ugly Caterpillar / by Carl Sommer; illustrated by Greg Budwine. -- 1 st ed.
  p. cm. -- (Another Sommer-Time Story)
 Summary: Speckles the spider and Crumbs the cricket think a caterpillar is too ugly to be their friend, but Annie the ant insists that something beautiful might be inside.
 Cover title: Carl Sommer's The Ugly Caterpillar.
 ISBN 1-57537-015-8 (hardcover: alk. paper). -- ISBN 1-57537-058-1 library binding: alk. paper)
 [1. Insects Fiction. 2. Beauty, Personal Fiction. 3. Conduct of life Fiction.] I. Budwine, Greg, ill. II. Title. III. Title: Carl Sommer's The Ugly Caterpillar. IV. Series: Sommer, Carl, 1930- Another Sommer-Time Story.
PZ7.S696235Ug 2000   99-35282
[E]--dc21   CIP

Speckles the spider, Annie the ant, and a crickety ol' cricket named Crumbs lived under a giant willow tree beside Crystal Lake.

The three friends had lots of fun running and hopping and playing together. They swung on the branches and slid down the leaves.

Sometimes they floated together in the lake on an old hollow branch.

One day while the three friends were playing
in the shade of the willow tree, Crumbs noticed
something strange. "Hurry up!" he shouted to

his friends. "Look what I've found!"

Annie and Speckles ran to see what had made Crumbs so excited.

"What is it?" asked Speckles.

Crumbs pointed to a yellow egg on a smooth, green leaf and said, "Look at this funny thing!"

"Oh!" exclaimed Annie. "I wonder what lives in there?"

"I don't know," said Speckles laughing, "but I bet it's ugly."

"Shhhhh!" said Annie.   "Don't say that! Something beautiful might be inside."

"Inside there?" scoffed Crumbs.   "Nothing beautiful could come from that ugly old egg."

For the rest of the day, Crumbs and Speckles laughed at Annie for what she had said.   They did not know what lived inside that egg, but they knew it had to be ugly!

Every day the three friends would climb up the tree and peek at the tiny yellow egg. They wanted to know what lived inside.

"Shhhhh!" said Annie. "Don't say that! Something beautiful might be inside."

"Inside there?" scoffed Crumbs. "Nothing beautiful could come from that ugly old egg."

For the rest of the day, Crumbs and Speckles laughed at Annie for what she had said. They did not know what lived inside that egg, but they knew it had to be ugly!

Every day the three friends would climb up the tree and peek at the tiny yellow egg. They wanted to know what lived inside.

One day, Crumbs reached the smooth, green
leaf before his friends. He saw a strange-looking
creature poking its head out of the egg.

"Quick!" yelled Crumbs. "Come look at this ugly worm."

Speckles and Annie raced across the branches.

"Oh!" exclaimed Annie. "It's a caterpillar."

"It sure is funny looking," said Crumbs.

"It's ugly!" said Speckles.

"No, it's not," insisted Annie. "Just because it's different doesn't make it ugly."

Speckles ignored Annie. "Remember when Annie said, 'Something beautiful might be inside'?"

Crumbs giggled. "Was she ever wrong!"

Speckles laughed and said, "She sure was!"

"Ha! Ha! Ha!" chuckled Crumbs. "That's the ugliest thing I've *ever* seen."

Then Speckles and Crumbs laughed so hard their insides began to hurt. But not Annie. She did not think it was the least bit funny.

Soon the three friends forgot all about the caterpillar. They went back to their favorite place to swing and climb and have lots of fun.

One day as the three friends were floating on
the lake, they happened to see a caterpillar on the
bank.

"Hello!" shouted the caterpillar. She politely
introduced herself. "I'm Katy. May I play, too?"

"Of course!" said Annie with a great big smile.
"Come float on the lake with us."

Immediately, Annie began rowing to shore.

"W-a-i-t just a minute!" shouted Crumbs. "We don't want you to play with us."

"Why not?" asked Katy very softly.

"Because...well." Speckles held back a laugh. "You're just too ugly."

"Look at you," laughed Crumbs. "You have six little arms and ten short legs. And you don't even have a neck! We'd be embarrassed to be seen with someone looking like you."

"I can't help the way I look," said Katy as she began to cry. "I was born this way."

"Sorry-y-y-y," answered Speckles and Crumbs. "You're much too ugly to be our friend."

"You're not ugly to me!" said Annie. She frowned at her rude friends and jumped onto the bank. "I'd love to be your friend."

Crumbs and Speckles giggled as Annie walked away with her funny-looking friend.

When they were alone, Katy asked, "Why am I so ugly?"

"You're not ugly just because someone else says so," answered Annie. "My parents say you can't tell if someone's ugly just by their looks."

"What do you mean?" asked Katy.

"What you look like on the outside isn't as important as what you look like on the inside," explained Annie. "Things like love and kindness, honesty and goodness—*those* are the important things that make someone beautiful."

"I feel so much better," said Katy. "I'm sure glad you're my friend."

"And I'm glad you're *my* friend, too," answered Annie.

"Let's get something to eat," said Katy. "I'm hungry."

From then on, Annie and Katy were the best of friends. They met every day and played together. After playing, they would climb up the willow tree and eat.

One day Annie got scared when she noticed something strange happening to her friend.

"Hey, what's happening to you?" asked Annie. "You're coming apart!"

"No, I'm not," laughed Katy. "When my skin gets too tight, I just grow some more. Then I get rid of the old skin."

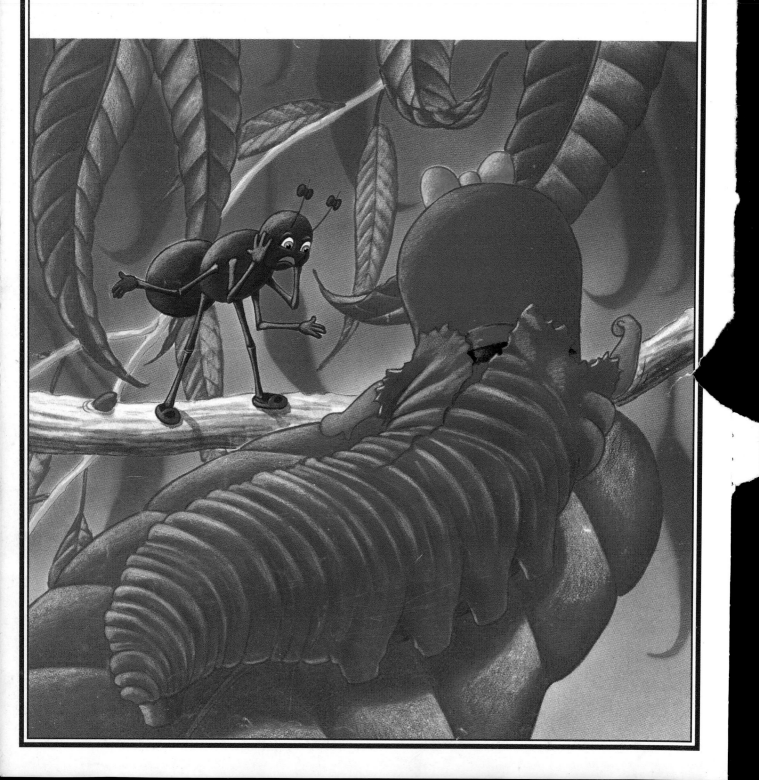

"Watch me," said Katy as she wiggled right out of her skin.

"Wow!" squeaked Annie. "I've never seen anything like that before."

"Oh, I just keep on doing this until I'm big and strong," explained Katy.

One day, Annie was having a great time playing with Katy on some leaves hanging over the lake. Suddenly, a strong gust of wind came. It blew Annie off the leaf.

Kerplop! Annie fell near a hungry fish. The fish started to swim towards Annie

"Help me! Help me!" screamed Annie. "A fish

Soon the three friends forgot all about the caterpillar. They went back to their favorite place to swing and climb and have lots of fun.

One day as the three friends were floating on the lake, they happened to see a caterpillar on the bank.

"Hello!" shouted the caterpillar. She politely introduced herself. "I'm Katy. May I play, too?"

"Of course!" said Annie with a great big smile. "Come float on the lake with us."

Immediately, Annie began rowing to shore.

is coming to swallow me up!"

Quickly, Katy chewed off a big leaf. The leaf
fell near Annie. Annie swished herself as fast as
she could toward the leaf and climbed aboard—
just in time.

Shaking all over, Annie said, "Whew! Was
that ever scary!"

Annie held on tightly as the wind blew her to shore. She jumped off the leaf and hurried back up the tree.

She hugged Katy and said, "Thank you! Thank you! You saved my life!"

Day after day Annie and Katy laughed and played together. Then it happened again—Katy shed her skin.

"My, my!" said Annie. "You're getting bigger and bigger, and you're looking so different. What's that thing poking out of your head?"

"It's a horn to scare away my enemies," replied Katy.

One day Katy said to Annie, "I have to leave for a few weeks."

Annie scratched her head. "Why?"

"Something really big is about to happen to me," answered Katy, "and I must find a safe place to stay. But don't worry, I'll be back soon."

"I'm going to miss you very much," said Annie, wiping tears from her eyes. "We had so much fun together."

"Don't be sad," said Katy as she began to leave. "When I come back, we'll have more fun than ever."

Annie waved goodbye as she watched her friend crawl away. Katy climbed high in the willow tree and tied herself to a branch.

Before long, Katy changed into a chrysalis. Every day, Annie went to see what was happening to her friend. Often she would call out, "Katy, are you okay?"

But Katy never answered. Annie hoped that her friend would return soon.

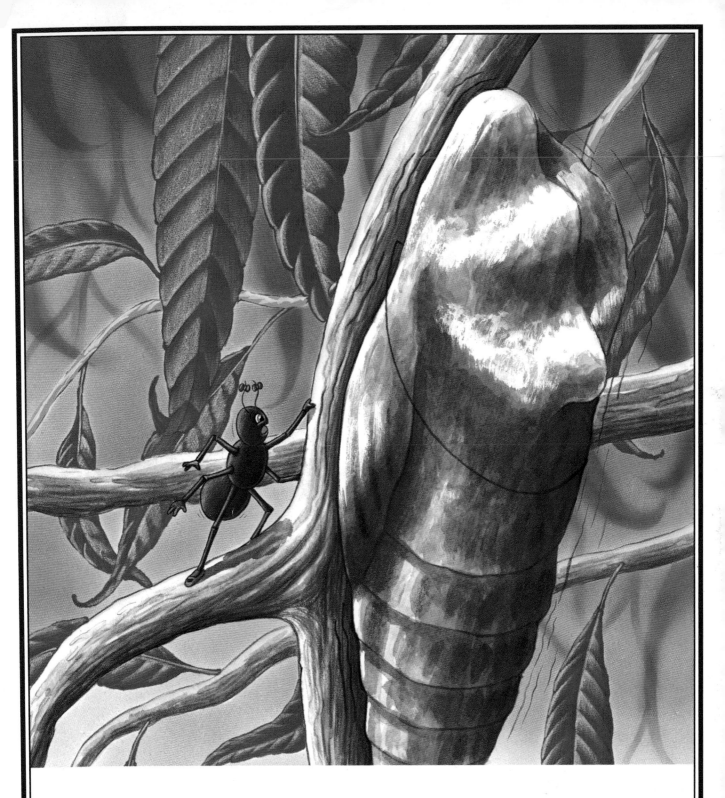

One day while Annie was watching the chrysalis, the whole thing began to shake.

"Oh no!" cried Annie. "What's happening to my friend Katy? Something must be wrong."

Annie put her head in her hands and began to cry.

All of a sudden the chrysalis began to crack. Then, as Annie watched in amazement, out popped a strange-looking head!

"Who are you?" demanded Annie. "And what have you done with my friend?"

"I *am* your friend, Katy the caterpillar. Only now I'm a butterfly."

"You're...you're who...uh, what?" asked Annie.

"I'm a butterfly now," grunted Katy as she jiggled and wiggled. "Wait until I get out of this chrysalis, and then I'll explain."

Annie could hardly speak. "Y-y-you look so different!"

"That's what happens to us butterflies," said Katy. "First we come from a small egg as a caterpillar. As we continue to grow, we keep shedding our skin. Then we turn into a chrysalis. And finally—TA DAH!—our bodies change into a butterfly."

"Wow!" exclaimed Annie. "You're beautiful!"

"Before I do anything else," said Katy, "let me dry myself in the warm sun."

"This is amazing!" said Annie, scratching her head. "If I hadn't seen it with my own eyes, I never would have believed it."

After drying her wings, Katy said, "Hop on my back, Annie. We'll go for a ride."

Up climbed Annie, and away they went.

Katy and Annie flew high above the trees and over Crystal Lake. They flew all around the countryside, visiting many wonderful places.

"This is fun up here!" shouted Annie.

Then they flew over Annie's home. From above the tree tops, Katy happened to see a spider and a crickety ol' cricket. "Look!" she yelled. "It's Speckles and Crumbs!"

"Let's go say hi," said Annie.

"Who's your new friend?" asked Speckles.

"She sure is pretty," added Crumbs. "We'd love to have her as our friend."

"It's Katy the caterpillar," laughed Annie.

"You can't fool us," scoffed Speckles.

"She's no ugly caterpillar," insisted Crumbs. "She's beautiful!"

Speckles walked over to the butterfly and sweetly asked, "Would you be our friend?"

"You want *me* to be *your* friend?" asked a surprised Katy.

"It's Katy!" blurted Crumbs. "It really is!"

Speckles put on a great big smile. "Now that you're so pretty, we'd love to be your friends."

"Why didn't you like me when I was a caterpillar?" asked Katy.

"W-w-well," stuttered Speckles.

Crumbs tried to explain. "We didn't know you would turn into such a beautiful butterfly."

"It shouldn't matter what someone looks like on the outside," answered Katy as she winked at Annie. "You never know—something beautiful might be on the inside."

Speckles and Crumbs lowered their heads.

Then Katy said to Annie, "Let's go and have some fun and fly again."

"I'm ready!" said Annie, giggling.

Katy began flapping her wings.

"Hey!" yelled Speckles. "What about us?"

"Yeah!" shouted Crumbs. "We like you now!"

"Sorry-y-y," Katy called back. "If you didn't like me when I was a caterpillar, you wouldn't like me now. I'm still the same on the inside."

"Oooohhhh!" moaned Speckles and Crumbs. They were mad at themselves for having treated Katy so badly.

"So long," said Annie and Katy as they waved
goodbye. In a flash they were on their way.
   Sadly, Speckles and Crumbs watched them
until they could see them no more.

Then Speckles turned slowly to Crumbs and groaned, "You know, Annie was right."

"She sure was," mumbled Crumbs. "Something beautiful *was* on the inside!"